Ladybugs Have Lots of Spots

Sheryl and Simon Shapiro

annick press
toronto + new york + vancouver

Annick Press Ltd.
All rights reserved. No part of this work covered by the copyrights hereon may be reproduced or used in any form or by any means—graphic, electronic, or mechanical—without the prior written permission of the publisher.

We acknowledge the support of the Canada Council for the Arts, the Ontario Arts Council, and the Government of Canada through the Canada Book Fund (CBF) for our publishing activities.

ONTARIO ARTS COUNCIL
CONSEIL DES ARTS DE L'ONTARIO
50 YEARS OF ONTARIO GOVERNMENT SUPPORT OF THE ARTS
50 ANS DE SOUTIEN DU GOUVERNEMENT DE L'ONTARIO AUX ARTS

Cataloging in Publication

Shapiro, Sheryl
    Ladybugs have lots of spots / Sheryl and Simon Shapiro.

(Shapes & spaces)
Issued also in electronic format.
ISBN 978-1-55451-557-8 (bound).—ISBN 978-1-55451-556-1 (pbk.)

    1. Circle—Juvenile literature. I. Shapiro, Simon II. Title
III. Series: Shapes & spaces.

BF293.S52 2013   j152.14'23   C2013-900593-5

Distributed in Canada by:
Firefly Books Ltd.
50 Staples Avenue, Unit 1
Richmond Hill, ON L4B 0A7

Published in the U.S.A. by Annick Press (U.S.) Ltd.
Distributed in the U.S.A. by:
Firefly Books (U.S.) Inc.
P.O. Box 1338
Ellicott Station
Buffalo, NY 14205

Printed in China

Visit us at: www.annickpress.com

Photo credits:

Cover and inside: ladybug on daisy and camomile with ladybug, © Konstantin Sutyagin/Bigstock.com and © Tiplyashin Anatoly/Bigstock.com; ladybug on die, © John Evans/Bigstock.com; buttons, © Eleonora Kolomiyets/Bigstock.com; lasso, © Olivier Le Queinec/Bigstock.com; hula hooping girl, © iStockphoto, Inc./Thomas_EyeDesign; sliding girl, © iStockphoto, Inc./Noam Armonn; boy in rubber ring, © Olga Demchishina/Dreamstime.com; girl in polka dot hat, © Elena Rostunova/Dreamstime.com; fruit used small throughout, © Valentyn Volkov/Bigstock.com; hands of senior woman holding walking sticks, © iStockphoto, Inc./ Slobodan Vasic; Siamese kitten, © Mark Hayes/Dreamstime.com; yellow car, © Simon Shapiro; traffic light, © Hank Shiffman/Bigstock.com; children in a circle, © Yuri Arcurs/Bigstock.com; crayons in a circle, © Lawrence Long/Bigstock.com; toy watering can, © Alexey Romanov/Bigstock.com; holey sock with smiley toe, © Eva Gruendemann/Bigstock.com; Ferris wheel, © Vitalliy/Dreamstime.com; girl on tricycle, © Thomas Perkins/Dreamstime.com; cylinder blocks, © Lori Sparkia/Bigstock.com; little chef, © Thomas Perkins/Bigstock.com; big Earth, © Cloki/Dreamstime.com; boy holding globe, © Jose Manuel Gelpi Diaz/Dreamstime.com; small Earth, © Kirill Kurashov/Bigstock.com; striped ball, © Windujedi/Dreamstime.com; DVD, pomegranate, ornament, compass, bagel, © Kirill Kurashov/Bigstock.com; green dish, © Oleg Saenko/Bigstock.com; cookie, © Vaide Seskauskiene/Bigstock.com; grapefruit, © Valentyn Volkov/Bigstock.com; basketball, © Dana Rothstein/Bigstock.com; back cover: feet, © Jasmin Merdan/Bigstock.com.

For our great-nephews
and great-nieces:
Paloma, Leo, Elisheva,
and Mickey—
great kids all!

Three round buttons,
one rope loop—

same shape as
a hula hoop.

Sliding sister,
wriggling brother,
in one side
and out the other.

Ladybugs have
lots of spots—

so do hats
with polka dots.

Rings are thin,
rings are fat,
on a finger,
on a cat.

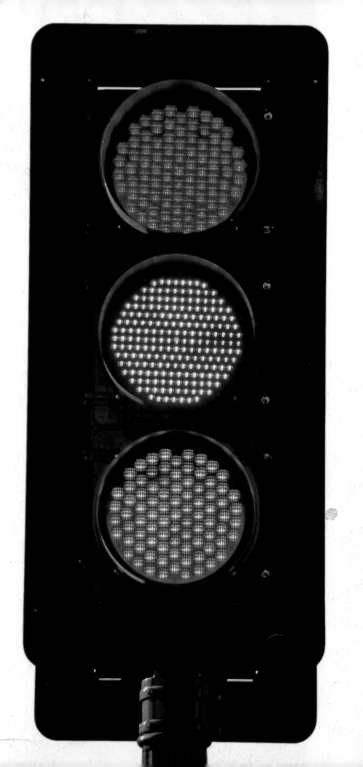

Round black tires,
lots of tread,
go on green
and stop on red.

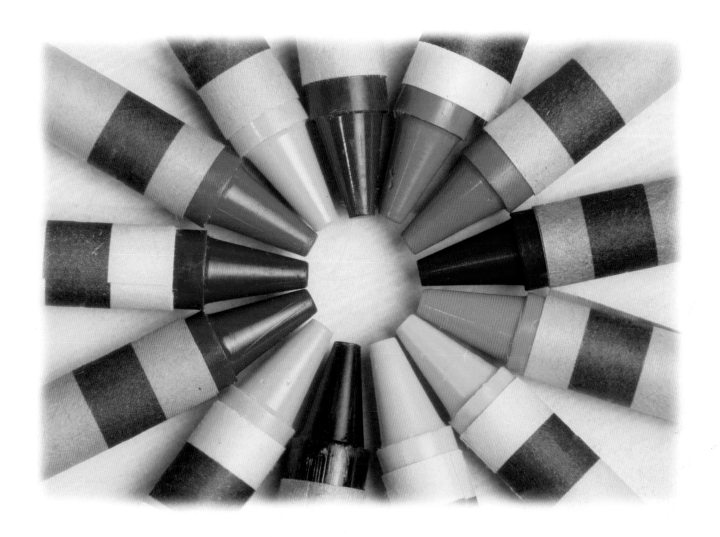

**Make a circle with your friends
or crayons touching at the ends.**

I like holes
where water flows,

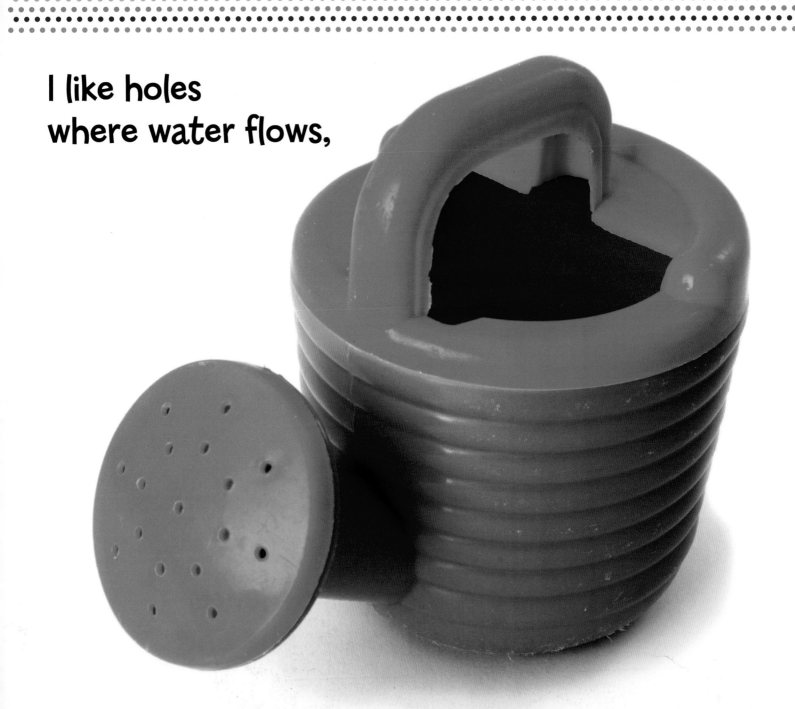

but not the ones that show my toes.

Spokes in wheels
spin round and round,
in the air
or on the ground.

A cylinder's
both round and flat—

the bottom of
a baker's hat!

Earth is shaped
just like a ball,
but Earth is big,
a globe is small.